Large Print Edition

FOUR YEARS

1887-1891

SPECIAL LARGE PRINT EDITION
with easy-to-read text

WILLIAM BUTLER YEATS

Serenity Publishers, LLC
ROCKVILLE, MARYLAND
2013

Four Years (Large Print Edition) by **William Butler Yeats** in its current format, copyright © Serenity Publishers 2013. This book, in whole or in part, may not be copied or reproduced in its current format by any means, electronic, mechanical or otherwise without the permission of the publisher.

The original text has been reformatted for clarity and to fit this edition.

Serenity Publishers & associated logos are trademarks or registered trademarks of Serenity Publishers, Rockville, Maryland. All other trademarks are properties of their respective owners.

This book is presented as is, without any warranties (implied or otherwise) as to the accuracy of the production, text or translation. The publisher does not take responsibility for any typesetting, formatting, translation or other errors which may have occurred during the production of this book.

ISBN: 978-1-61242-839-0

Published by Serenity Publishers
An Arc Manor Company
P. O. Box 10339
Rockville, MD 20849-0339
www.SerenityPublishers.com

Printed in the United States of America/United Kingdom

FOUR YEARS 1887-1891

At the end of the eighties my father and mother, my brother and sisters and myself, all newly arrived from Dublin, were settled in Bedford Park in a red-brick house with several wood mantlepieces copied from marble mantlepieces by the brothers Adam, a balcony, and a little garden shadowed by a great horse-chestnut tree. Years before we had lived there, when the crooked, ostentatiously picturesque streets, with sgreat trees casting great shadows, had been anew enthusiasm: the Pre-Raphaelite movement at last affecting life. But now exaggerated criticism had taken the place of enthusiasm; the tiled roofs, the first in modern London, were said to leak, which they did not, & the drains to be bad, though that was no longer true; and I imagine that houses were cheap. I remember feeling disappointed because the co-operative stores, with their little seventeenth century panes, were so like any

3

common shop; and because the public house, called 'The Tabard' after Chaucer's Inn, was so plainly a common public house; and because the great sign of a trumpeter designed by Rooke, the Pre- Raphaelite artist, had been freshened by some inferior hand. The big red-brick church had never pleased me, and I was accustomed, when I saw the wooden balustrade that ran along the slanting edge of the roof, where nobody ever walked or could walk, to remember the opinion of some architect friend of my father's, that it had been put there to keep the birds from falling off. Still, however, it had some village characters and helped us to feel not wholly lost in the metropolis. I no longer went to church as a regular habit, but go I sometimes did, for one Sunday morning I saw these words painted on a board in the porch: 'The congregation are requested to kneel during prayers; the kneelers are afterwards to be hung upon pegs provided for the purpose.' In front of every seat hung a little cushion, and these cushions were called 'kneelers.' Presently the joke ran through the community, where there were many artists, who considered religion at best an unimportant accessory to good architecture and who disliked that particular church.

II

I could not understand where the charm had gone that I had felt, when as a school-boy of twelve or thirteen, I had played among the unfinished houses, once leaving the marks of my two hands, blacked by a fall among some paint, upon a white balustrade. Sometimes I thought it was because these were real houses, while my play had been among toy-houses some day to be inhabited by imaginary people full of the happiness that one can see in picture books. I was in all things Pre-Raphaelite. When I was fifteen or sixteen, my father had told me about Rossetti and Blake and given me their poetry to read; & once in Liverpool on my way to Sligo, "I had seen 'Dante's Dream' in the gallery there—a picture painted when Rossetti had lost his dramatic power, and to-day not very pleasing to me—and its colour, its people, its romantic architecture had blotted all other pictures away." It was a perpetual bewilderment that my father, who had begun life as a Pre-Raphaelite painter, now painted portraits of the first comer, children selling newspapers, or a consumptive girl with a basket offish upon her head, and that when, moved perhaps by memory of his youth, he chose some theme from poetic tradition, he would soon weary and leave it unfinished. I had seen the change coming bit by bit and its defence elaborated by young men fresh from the Paris art- schools. 'We must paint what is in front of us,' or 'A man must be of his own time,' they would say, and if I spoke of Blake or Rossetti they would point out his bad drawing and tell me to admire Carolus Duran and Bastien-Lepage. Then, too, they were very ignorant men; they read nothing, for nothing mattered but 'Knowing how to paint,' being in reaction against a generation that seemed to have wasted its time upon so many things. I thought myself alone in hating these young men, now indeed getting towards middle life, their contempt for the past, their monopoly of the future, but in a few months I was to discover others of my own age, who thought as I did, for it is not true that youth looks before it with the mechanical gaze of a well-drilled soldier. Its quarrel is not with the past, but with the present, where its elders are so obviously powerful, and no cause seems lost if it seem to threaten that power. Does cultivated youth ever really love the future, where the eye can discover no persecuted Royalty hidden among oak leaves, though from it certainly does come so much proletarian rhetoric? I was unlike others of my generation in one thing only. I am very religious, and deprived by Huxley and Tyndall, whom I detested, of the simple-minded religion of my childhood, I had made a new religion, almost an infallible church, out of poetic tradition: a fardel of stories, and of personages, and of emotions, a bundle of images and of masks passed on from generation to generation by poets & painters with some help from philosophers and theologians. I wished for a world where I could discover this tradition perpetually, and not in pictures and in poems only, but in tiles round the chimney-piece and in the hangings that kept out the draught. I had even created a dogma: 'Because those imaginary people are created out of the deepest instinct of man, to be his measure and his norm, whatever I can imagine those mouths speaking may be the nearest I can go to truth.' When I listened they seemed always to speak of one thing only: they, their loves, every incident of their lives, were steeped in the supernatural. Could even Titian's 'Ariosto' that I loved beyond other portraits, have its grave look, as if waiting for some perfect final event, if the painters, before Titian, had not learned portraiture, while

7

painting into the corner of compositions, full of saints and Madonnas, their kneeling patrons? At seventeen years old I was already an old-fashioned brass cannon full of shot, and nothing kept me from going off but a doubt as to my capacity to shoot straight.

III

I was not an industrious student and knew only what I had found by accident, and I had found "nothing I cared for after Titian—and Titian I knew chiefly from a copy of 'the supper of Emmaus' in Dublin—till Blake and the Pre-Raphaelites;" and among my father's friends were no Pre-Raphaelites. Some indeed had come to Bedford Park in the enthusiasm of the first building, and others to be near those that had. There was Todhunter, a well-off man who had bought my father's pictures while my father was still Pre- Raphaelite. Once a Dublin doctor he was a poet and a writer of poetical plays: a tall, sallow, lank, melancholy man, a good scholar and a good intellect; and with him my father carried on a warm exasperated friendship, fed I think by old memories and wasted by quarrels over matters of opinion. Of all the survivors he was the most dejected, and the least estranged, and I remember encouraging him, with a sense of worship shared, to buy a very expensive carpet designed by Morris. He displayed it without strong liking and would have agreed had there been any to find fault. If he had liked anything strongly he might have been a famous man, for a few years later he was to write, under some casual patriotic impulse, certain excellent verses now in all Irish anthologies; but with him every book was a new planting and not a new bud on an old bough. He had I think no peace in himself. But my father's chief friend was York Powell, a famous Oxford Professor of history, a broad-built, broad-headed, brown-bearded man, clothed in heavy blue cloth and looking, but for his glasses and the dim sight of a student, like some captain in the merchant service. One often passed with pleasure from Todhunter's company to that of one who was almost ostentatiously at peace. He cared nothing for philosophy, nothing for economics, nothing for the policy of nations, for history, as he saw it, was a memory of men who were amusing or exciting to think about. He impressed all who met him & seemed to some a man of genius, but he had not enough ambition to shape his thought, or conviction to give rhythm to his style, and remained always a poor writer. I was too full of unfinished speculations and premature convictions to value rightly his conversation, in-formed by a vast erudition, which would give itself to every casual association of speech and company precisely because he had neither cause nor design. My father, however, found Powell's concrete narrative manner a necessary completion of his own; and when I asked him, in a letter many years later, where he got his philosophy, replied 'From York Powell' and thereon added, no doubt remembering that Powell was without ideas, 'By looking at him.' Then there was a good listener, a painter in whose hall hung a big picture, painted in his student days, of Ulysses sailing home from the Phaeacian court, an orange and a skin of wine at his side, blue mountains towering behind; but who lived by drawing domestic scenes and lovers' meetings for a weekly magazine that had an immense circulation among the imperfectly educated. To escape the boredom of work, which he never turned to but under pressure of necessity, and usually late at night with the publisher's messenger in the hall, he had half filled his studio with mechanical toys of his own invention, and perpetually increased their number. A model railway train at intervals puffed its way along the walls, passing several railway stations and signal boxes; and on the floor lay a camp with attacking and defending soldiers and a fortification that blew up when the attackers fired a pea through a certain window; while a large model of a Thames barge hung from the ceiling. Opposite our house lived an old artist who worked also for the illustrated papers for a living, but painted landscapes for his pleasure, and of him I remember nothing except that he had outlived ambition, was a good listener, and that my father explained his gaunt appearance by his descent from Pocahontas. If all these men were a little like becalmed ships, there was certainly one man whose sails were full. Three or four doors off, on our side of the road, lived a decorative artist in all the naive confidence of popular ideals and the public approval. He was our daily comedy. 'I myself and Sir Frederick Leighton are the greatest decorative artists of the age,' was among his sayings, & a great lych-gate, bought from some country church-yard, reared its thatched roof, meant to shelter bearers and coffin, above the entrance to his front garden, to show that he at any rate knew nothing of discouragement. In this fairly numerous company—there were others though no other face rises before me—my father and York Powell found listeners for a conversation that had no special loyalties, or antagonisms; while I could only talk upon set topics, being in the heat of my youth, and the topics that filled me with excitement were never spoken of.

IV

Some quarter of an hour's walk from Bedford Park, out on the high road to Richmond, lived W. E. Henley, and I, like many others, began under him my education. His portrait, a lithograph by Rothenstein, hangs over my mantlepiece among portraits of other friends. He is drawn standing, but, because doubtless of his crippled legs, he leans forward, resting his elbows upon some slightly suggested object—a table or a window-sill. His heavy figure and powerful head, the disordered hair standing upright, his short irregular beard and moustache, his lined and wrinkled face, his eyes steadily fixed upon some object, in complete confidence and self-possession, and yet as in half-broken reverie, all are exactly as I remember him. I have seen other portraits and they too show him exactly as I remember him, as though he had but one appearance and that seen fully at the first glance and by all alike. He was most human—

human, I used to say, like one of Shakespeare's characters—and yet pressed and pummelled, as it were, into a single attitude, almost into a gesture and a speech, as by some overwhelming situation. I disagreed with him about everything, but I admired him beyond words. With the exception of some early poems founded upon old French models, I disliked his poetry, mainly because he wrote *Vers Libre*, which I associated with Tyndall and Huxley and Bastien-Lepage's clownish peasant staring with vacant eyes at her great boots; and filled it with unimpassioned description of an hospital ward where his leg had been amputated. I wanted the strongest passions, passions that had nothing to do with observation, and metrical forms that seemed old enough to be sung by men half-asleep or riding upon a journey. Furthermore, Pre-Raphaelitism affected him as some people are affected by a cat in the room, and though he professed himself at our first meeting without political interests or convictions, he soon grew into a violent unionist and imperialist. I used to say when I spoke of his poems: 'He is like a great actor with a bad part; yet who would look at Hamlet in the grave scene if Salvini played the grave-digger?' and I might so have explained much that he said and did. I meant that he was like a great actor of passion—character-acting meant nothing to me for many years—and an actor of passion will display some one quality of soul, personified again and again, just as a great poetical painter, Titian, Botticelli, Rossetti may depend for his greatness upon a type of beauty which presently we call by his name. Irving, the last of the sort on the English stage, and in modern England and France it is the rarest sort, never moved me but in the expression of intellectual pride; and though I saw Salvini but once, I am convinced that his genius was a kind of animal nobility. Henley, half inarticulate—'I am very costive,' he would say—beset with personal quarrels, built up an image of power and magnanimity till it became, at moments, when seen as it were by lightning, his true self. Half his opinions were the contrivance of a sub-consciousness that sought always to bring life to the dramatic crisis, and expression to that point of artifice where the true self could find its tongue. Without opponents there had been no drama, and in his youth Ruskinism and Pre-Raphaelitism, for he was of my father's generation, were the only possible opponents. How could one resent his prejudice when, that he himself might play a worthy part, he must find beyond the common rout, whom he derided and flouted daily, opponents he could imagine moulded like himself? Once he said to me in the height of his imperial propaganda, 'Tell those young men in Ireland that this great thing must go on. They say Ireland is not fit for self-government but that is nonsense. It is as fit as any other European country but we cannot grant it.' And then he spoke of his desire to found and edit a Dublin newspaper. It would have expounded the Gaelic propaganda then beginning, though Dr. Hyde had as yet no league, our old stories, our modern literature—everything that did not demand any shred or patch of government. He dreamed of a tyranny but it was that of Cosimo de Medici.

V

We gathered on Sunday evenings in two rooms, with folding doors between, & hung, I think, with photographs from Dutch masters, and in one room there was always, I think, a table with cold meat. I can recall but one elderly man—Dunn his name was—rather silent and full of good sense, an old friend of Henley's. We were young men, none as yet established in his own, or in the world's opinion, and Henley was our leader and our confidant. One evening I found him alone amused and exasperated.

He cried: 'Young A... has just been round to ask my advice. Would I think it a wise thing if he bolted with Mrs. B...? "Have you quite determined to do it?" I asked him. "Quite." "Well," I said, "in that case I refuse to give you any advice."' Mrs. B... was a beautiful talented woman, who, as the Welsh triad said of Guinevere, 'was much given to being carried off.' I think we listened to him, and often obeyed him, partly because he was quite plainly not upon the side of our parents. We might have a different ground of quarrel, but the result seemed more important than the ground, and his confident manner and speech made us believe, perhaps for the first time, in victory. And besides, if he did denounce, and in my case he certainly did, what we held in secret reverence, he never failed to associate it with things, or persons, that did not move us to reverence. Once I found him just returned from some art congress in Liverpool or in Manchester. 'The Salvation Armyism of art,' he called it, & gave a grotesque description of some city councillor he had found admiring Turner. Henley, who hated all that Ruskin praised, thereupon derided Turner, and finding the city councillor the next day on the other side of the gallery, admiring some Pre-Raphaelite there, derided that Pre-Raphaelite. The third day Henley discovered the poor man on a chair in the middle of the room, staring disconsolately upon the floor. He terrified us also, and certainly I did not dare, and I think none of us dared, to speak our admiration for book or picture he condemned, but he made us feel always our importance, and no man among us could do good work, or show the promise of it, and lack his praise.

I can remember meeting of a Sunday night Charles Whibley, Kenneth Grahame, author of 'The Golden Age,' Barry Pain, now a well known novelist, R. A. M. Stevenson, art critic and a famous talker, George Wyndham, later on a cabinet minister and Irish chief secretary, and Oscar Wilde, who was some eight years or ten older than the rest. But faces and names are vague to me and, while faces that I met but once may rise clearly before me, a face met on many a Sunday has perhaps vanished. Kipling came sometimes, I think, but I never met him; and Stepniak, the nihilist, whom I knew well elsewhere but not there, said 'I cannot go more than once a year, it is too exhausting.' Henley got the best out of us all, because he had made us accept him as our judge and we knew that his judgment could neither sleep, nor be softened, nor changed, nor turned aside. When I think of him, the antithesis that is the foundation of human nature being ever in my sight, I see his crippled legs as though he were some Vulcan perpetually forging swords for other men to use; and certainly I always thought of C..., a fine classical scholar, a pale and seemingly gentle man, as our chief swordsman and bravo. When Henley founded his weekly newspaper, first the 'Scots,' afterwards 'The National Observer,' this young man wrote articles and reviews notorious for savage wit; and years afterwards when 'The National Observer' was dead, Henley dying & our cavern of outlaws empty, I met him in Paris very sad and I think very poor. 'Nobody will employ me now,' he said. 'Your master is gone,' I answered, 'and you are like the spear in an old Irish story that had to be kept dipped in poppy- juice that it might not go about killing people on its own account.' I wrote my first good lyrics and tolerable essays for 'The National Obsever' and as I always signed my work could go my own road in some measure. Henley often revised my lyrics, crossing out a line or a stanza and writing in one of his own, and I was comforted by my belief that he also re-wrote Kipling then in the first flood of popularity. At first, indeed, I was ashamed of being re-written and thought that others were not, and only began investigation when the editorial characteristics—epigrams, archaisms and all—appeared in the article upon Paris fashions and in that upon opium by an Egyptian Pasha. I was not compelled to full conformity for verse is plainly stubborn; and in prose, that I might avoid unacceptable opinions, I wrote nothing but ghost or fairy stories, picked up from my mother, or some pilot at Rosses Point, and Henley saw that I must needs mix a palette fitted to my subject matter. But if he had changed every 'has' into 'hath' I would have let him, for had not we sunned ourselves in his generosity? 'My young men out-dome and they write better than I,' he wrote in some letter praising Charles Whibley's work, and to another friend with a copy of my 'Man who dreamed of Fairyland:' 'See what a fine thing has been written by one of my lads.'

VI

My first meeting with Oscar Wilde was an astonishment. I never before heard a man talking with perfect sentences, as if he had written them all over night with labour and yet all spontaneous. There was present that night at Henley's, by right of propinquity or of accident, a man full of the secret spite of dullness, who interrupted from time to time and always to check or disorder thought; and I noticed with what mastery he was foiled and thrown. I noticed, too, that the impression of artificiality that I think all Wilde's listeners have recorded, came from the perfect rounding of the sentences and from the deliberation that made it possible. That very impression helped him as the effect of metre, or of the antithetical prose of the seventeenth century, which is itself a true metre, helps a writer, for he could pass without incongruity from some unforeseen swift stroke of wit to elaborate reverie. I heard him say a few nights later: 'Give me "The Winter's Tale," "Daffodils that come before the swallow dare" but not "King Lear." What is "King Lear" but poor life staggering in the fog?' and the slow cadence, modulated with so great precision, sounded natural to my ears. That first night he praised Walter Pater's 'Essays on the Renaissance:' 'It is my golden book; I never travel anywhere without it; but it is the very flower of decadence. The last trumpet should have sounded the moment it was written.' 'But,' said the dull man, 'would you not have given us time to read it?' 'Oh no,' was the retort, 'there would have been plenty of time afterwards—in either world.' I think he seemed to us, baffled as we were by youth, or by infirmity, a triumphant figure, and to some of us a figure from another age, an audacious Italian fifteenth century figure. A few weeks before I had heard one of my father's friends, an official in a publishing firm that had employed both Wilde and Henley as editors, blaming Henley who was 'no use except under control' and praising Wilde, 'so indolent but such a genius;' and now the firm became the topic of our talk. 'How often do you go to the office?' said Henley. 'I used to go three times a week,' said Wilde, 'for an hour a day but I have since struck off one of the days.' 'My God,' said Henley, 'I went five times a week for five hours a day and when I wanted to strike off a day they had a special committee meeting.' 'Furthermore,' was Wilde's answer, 'I never answered their letters. I have known men come to London full of bright prospects and seen them complete wrecks in a few months through a habit of answering letters.' He too knew how to keep our elders in their place, and his method was plainly the more successful for Henley had been dismissed. 'No he is not an aesthete,' Henley commented later, being somewhat embarrassed by Wilde's Pre-Raphaelite entanglement. 'One soon finds that he is a scholar and a gentleman.' And when I dined with Wilde a few days afterwards he began at once, 'I had to strain every nerve to equal that man at all;' and I was too loyal to speak my thought: 'You & not he' said all the brilliant things. He like the rest of us had felt the strain of an intensity that seemed to hold life at the point of drama. He had said, on that first meeting, 'The basis of literary friendship is mixing the poisoned bowl;' and for a few weeks Henley and he became close friends till, the astonishment of their meeting over, diversity of character and ambition pushed them apart, and, with half the cavern helping, Henley began mixing the poisoned bowl for Wilde. Yet Henley never wholly lost that first admiration, for after Wilde's downfall he said to me: 'Why did he do it? I told my lads to attack him and yet we might have fought under his banner.'

VII

It became the custom, both at Henley's and at Bedford Park, to say that R. A. M. Stevenson, who frequented both circles, was the better talker. Wilde had been trussed up like a turkey by undergraduates, dragged up and down a hill, his champagne emptied into the ice tub, hooted in the streets of various towns and I think stoned, and no newspaper named him but in scorn; his manner had hardened to meet opposition and at times he allowed one to see an unpardonable insolence. His charm was acquired and systematised, a mask which he wore only when it pleased him, while the charm of Stevenson belonged to him like the colour of his hair. If Stevenson's talk became monologue we did not know it, because our one object was to show by our attention that he need never leave off. If thought failed him we would not combat what he had said, or start some new theme, but would encourage him with

25

a question; and one felt that it had been always so from childhood up. His mind was full of phantasy for phantasy's sake and he gave as good entertainment in monologue as his cousin Robert Louis in poem or story. He was always 'supposing:' 'Suppose you had two millions what would you do with it?' and 'Suppose you were in Spain and in love how would you propose?' I recall him one afternoon at our house at Bedford Park, surrounded by my brother and sisters and a little group of my father's friends, describing proposals in half a dozen countries. There your father did it, dressed in such and such a way with such and such words, and there a friend must wait for the lady outside the chapel door, sprinkle her with holy water and say 'My friend Jones is dying for love of you.' But when it was over, those quaint descriptions, so full of laughter and sympathy, faded or remained in the memory as something alien from one's own life like a dance I once saw in a great house, where beautifully dressed children wound a long ribbon in and out as they danced. I was not of Stevenson's party and mainly I think because he had written a book in praise of Velasquez, praise at that time universal wherever Pre-Raphaelitism was accurst, and to my mind, that had to pick its symbols where its ignorance permitted, Velasquez seemed the first bored celebrant of boredom. I was convinced, from some obscure meditation, that

Stevenson's conversational method had joined him to my elders and to the indifferent world, as though it were right for old men, and unambitious men and all women, to be content with charm and humour. It was the prerogative of youth to take sides and when Wilde said: 'Mr. Bernard Shaw has no enemies but is intensely disliked by all his friends,' I knew it to be a phrase I should never forget, and felt revenged upon a notorious hater of romance, whose generosity and courage I could not fathom.

VIII

I saw a good deal of Wilde at that time—was it 1887 or 1888?—I have no way of fixing the date except that I had published my first book 'The Wanderings of Usheen' and that Wilde had not yet published his 'Decay of Lying.' He had, before our first meeting, reviewed my book and despite its vagueness of intention, and the inexactness of its speech, praised without qualification; and what was worth more than any review had talked about it, and now he asked me to eat my Xmas dinner with him, believing, I imagine, that I was alone in London.

He had just renounced his velveteen, and even those cuffs turned backward over the sleeves, and had begun to dress very carefully in the fashion of the moment. He lived in a little house at Chelsea that the architect Godwin had decorated with an elegance that owed something to Whistler. There was nothing mediaeval, nor Pre-Raphaelite, no cupboard door with figures upon flat gold, no peacock blue, no dark background. I remember vaguely a white drawing room with Whistler etchings, 'let in' to white panels, and a dining room all white: chairs, walls, mantlepiece, carpet, except for a diamond-shaped piece of red cloth in the middle of the table under a terra cotta statuette, and I think a red shaded lamp hanging from the ceiling to a little above the statuette. It was perhaps too perfect in its unity, his past of a few years before had gone too completely, and I remember thinking that the perfect harmony of his life there, with his beautiful wife and his two young children, suggested some deliberate artistic composition.

He commended, & dispraised himself, during dinner by attributing characteristics like his own to his country: 'We Irish are too poetical to be poets; we are a nation of brilliant failures, but we are the greatest talkers since the Greeks.' When dinner was over he read me from the proofs of 'The Decay of Lying' and when he came to the sentence: 'Schopenhauer has analysed the pessimism that characterises modern thought, but Hamlet invented it. The world has become sad because a puppet was once melancholy,' I said, 'Why do you change "sad" to "melancholy?"' He replied that he

29

wanted a full sound at the close of his sentence, and I thought it no excuse and an example of the vague impressiveness that spoilt his writing for me. Only when he spoke, or when his writing was the mirror of his speech, or in some simple fairytale, had he words exact enough to hold a subtle ear. He alarmed me, though not as Henley did for I never left his house thinking myself fool or dunce. He flattered the intellect of every man he liked; he made me tell him long Irish stories and compared my art of story-telling to Homer's; and once when he had described himself as writing in the census paper 'age 19, profession genius, infirmity talent,' the other guest, a young journalist fresh from Oxford or Cambridge, said 'What should I have written?' and was told that it should have been 'profession talent, infirmity genius.' When, however, I called, wearing shoes a little too yellow—unblackened leather had just become fashionable—I understood their extravagence when I saw his eyes fixed upon them; an another day Wilde asked me to tell his little boy a fairy story, and I had but got as far as 'Once upon a time there was a giant' when the little boy screamed and ran out of the room. Wilde looked grave and I was plunged into the shame of clumsiness that afflicts the young. When I asked for some literary gossip for some provincial newspaper, that paid me a few shillings a month, he explained very explicitly that writing literary gossip was no job for a gentleman. Though to be compared to Homer passed the time pleasantly, I had not been greatly perturbed had he stopped me with 'Is it a long story?' as Henley would certainly have done. I was abashed before him as wit and man of the world alone. I remember that he deprecated the very general belief in his success or his efficiency, and I think with sincerity. One form of success had gone: he was no more the lion of the season, and he had not discovered his gift for writing comedy, yet I think I knew him at the happiest moment of his life. No scandal had darkened his fame, his fame as a talker was growing among his equals, & he seemed to live in the enjoyment of his own spontaneity. One day he began: 'I have been inventing a Christian heresy,' and he told a detailed story, in the style of some early father, of how Christ recovered after the Crucifixion and, escaping from the tomb, lived on for many years, the one man upon earth who knew the falsehood of Christianity. Once St. Paul visited his town and he alone in the carpenters' quarter did not go to hear him preach. The other carpenters noticed that henceforth, for some unknown reason, he kept his hands covered. A few days afterwards I found Wilde, with smock frocks in various colours spread out upon the floor in front of him, while a missionary explained that he did not object to the heathen going naked upon week days, but insisted upon clothes in church. He had brought the smock frocks in a cab that the only art-critic whose fame had reached Central Africa might select a colour; so Wilde sat there weighing all with a conscious ecclesiastic solemnity.

VIII *(continued)*

Of late years I have often explained Wilde to myself by his family history. His father, was a friend or acquaintance of my father's father and among my family traditions there is an old Dublin riddle: 'Why are Sir William Wilde's nails so black?' Answer, 'Because he has scratched himself.' And there is an old story still current in Dublin of Lady Wilde saying to a servant. 'Why do you put the plates on the coal-scuttle? What are the chairs meant for?' They were famous people and there are many like stories, and even a horrible folk story, the invention of some Connaught peasant, that tells how Sir William Wilde took out the eyes of some men, who had come to consult him as an oculist, and laid them upon a plate, intending to replace them in a moment, and how the eyes were eaten by a cat. As a certain friend of mine, who has made a prolonged study of the nature of cats, said when he first heard the tale, 'Catslove eyes.' The Wilde family was clearly of the sort that fed the imagination of Charles Lever, dirty, untidy, daring, and what Charles Lever, who loved more normal activities, might not have valued so highly, very imaginative and learned. Lady Wilde, who when I knew her received her friends with blinds drawn and shutters closed that none might see her withered face, longed always perhaps, though certainly amid much self mockery, for some impossible splendour of character and circumstance. She lived near her son in level Chelsea, but I have heard her say, 'I want to live on some high place, Primrose Hill or Highgate, because I was an eagle in my youth.' I think her son lived with no self mockery at all an imaginary life; perpetually performed a play which was in all things the opposite of all that he had known in childhood and early youth; never put off completely his wonder at opening his eyes every morning on his own beautiful house, and in remembering that he had dined yesterday with a duchess and that he delighted in Flaubert and Pater, read Homer in the original and not as a school-master reads him for the grammar. I think, too, that because of all that half-civilized blood in his veins, he could not endure the sedentary toil of creative art and so remained a man of action, exaggerating, for the sake of immediate effect, every trick learned from his masters, turning their easel painting into painted scenes. He was a parvenu, but a parvenu whose whole bearing proved that if he did dedicate every story in 'The House of Pomegranates' to a lady of title, it was but to show that he was Jack and the social ladder his pantomime beanstalk. "Did you ever hear him say 'Marquess of Dimmesdale'?" a friend of his once asked me. "He does not say 'the Duke of York' with any pleasure."

He told me once that he had been offered a safe seat in Parliament and, had he accepted, he might have had a career like that of Beaconsfield, whose early style resembles his, being meant for crowds, for excitement, for hurried decisions, for immediate triumphs. Such men get their sincerity, if at all, from the contact of events; the dinner table was Wilde's event and made him the greatest talker of his time, and his plays and dialogues have what merit they possess from being now an imitation, now a record, of his talk. Even in those days I would often defend him by saying that his very admiration for his predecessors in poetry, for Browning, for Swinburne and Rossetti, in their first vogue while he was a very young man, made any success seem impossible that could satisfy his immense ambition: never but once before had the artist seemed so great, never had the work of art seemed so difficult. I would then compare him with Benvenuto Cellini who, coming after Michael Angelo, found nothing left to do so satisfactory as to turn bravo and assassinate the man who broke Michael Angelo's nose.

IX

I cannot remember who first brought me to the old stable beside Kelmscott House, William Morris' house at Hammersmith, & to the debates held there upon Sunday evenings by the socialist League. I was soon of the little group who had supper with Morris afterwards. I met at these suppers very constantly Walter Crane, Emery Walker presently, in association with Cobden Sanderson, the printer of many fine books, and less constantly Bernard Shaw and Cockerell, now of the museum of Cambridge, and perhaps but once or twice Hyndman the socialist and the anarchist Prince Krapotkin. There too one always met certain more or less educated workmen, rough of speech and manner, with a conviction to meet every turn. I was told by one of them, on a night when I had done perhaps more than my share of the talking, that I had talked more nonsense in one evening than he had heard in the whole course of his past life. I had merely preferred Parnell, then at the height of his career, to Michael Davitt who had wrecked his Irish influence by international politics. We sat round a long unpolished and unpainted trestle table of new wood in a room where hung Rossetti's 'Pomegranate,' a portrait of Mrs. Morris, and where one wall and part of the ceiling were covered by a great Persian carpet. Morris had said somewhere or other that carpets were meant for people who took their shoes off when they entered a house, and were most in place upon a tent floor. I was a little disappointed in the house, for Morris was an old man content at last to gather beautiful things rather than to arrange a beautiful house. I saw the drawing-room once or twice and there alone all my sense of decoration, founded upon the background of Rossetti's pictures, was satisfied by a big cupboard painted with a scene from Chaucer by Burne Jones, but even there were objects, perhaps a chair or a little table, that seemed accidental, bought hurriedly perhaps, and with little thought, to make wife or daughter comfortable. I had read as a boy in books belonging to my father, the third volume of 'The Earthly Paradise' and 'The Defence of Guinevere,' which pleased me less, but had not opened either for a long time. 'The man who never laughed again' had seemed the most wonderful of tales till my father had accused me of preferring Morris to Keats, got angry about it and put me altogether out of countenance. He had spoiled my pleasure, for now I questioned while I read and at last ceased to read; nor had Morris written as yet those prose romances that became, after his death, so great a joy that they were the only books I was ever to read slowly that I might not come too quickly to the end. It was now Morris himself that stirred my interest, and I took to him first because of some little tricks of speech and body that reminded me of my old grandfather in Sligo, but soon discovered his spontaneity and joy and made him my chief of men. To-day I do not set his poetry very high, but for an odd altogether wonderful line, or thought; and yet, if some angel offered me the choice, I would choose to live his life, poetry and all, rather than my own or any other man's. A reproduction of his portrait by Watts hangs over my mantlepiece with Henley's, and those of other friends. Its grave wide-open eyes, like the eyes of some dreaming beast, remind me of the open eyes of Titian's' Ariosto,' while the broad vigorous body suggests a mind that has no need of the intellect to remain sane, though it give itself to every phantasy, the dreamer of the middle ages. It is 'the fool of fairy ... wide and wild as a hill,' the resolute European image that yet half remembers Buddha's motionless meditation, and has no trait in common with the wavering, lean image of hungry speculation, that cannot but fill the mind's eye because of certain famous Hamlets of our stage. Shakespeare himself foreshadowed a symbolic change, that shows a change in the whole temperament of the world, for though he called his Hamlet 'fat, and scant of breath,' he thrust between his fingers agile rapier and dagger.

The dream world of Morris was as much the antithesis of daily life as with other men of genius, but he was never conscious of the antithesis and so knew nothing of intellectual suffering. His intellect, unexhausted by speculation or casuistry, was wholly at the service of hand and eye, and whatever he pleased he did with an unheard of ease and simplicity, and if style and vocabulary were at times monotonous, he could not have made them otherwise without ceasing to be himself. Instead of the language of Chaucer and Shakespeare, its warp fresh from field and market, if the woof were learned, his age offered him a speech, exhausted from abstraction, that only returned to its full vitality when written learnedly and slowly. The roots of his antithetical dream were visible enough: a never idle man of great physical strength and extremely irascible—did he not fling a badly baked plum pudding through the window upon Xmas Day?—a man more joyous than any intellectual man of our world, called himself 'the idle singer of an empty day' created new forms of melancholy, and faint persons, like the knights & ladies of Burne Jones, who are never, no, not once in forty volumes, put out of temper. A blunderer, who had said to the only unconverted man at a socialist picnic in Dublin, to prove that equality came easy, 'I was brought up a gentleman and now, as you can see, associate with all sorts,' and left wounds thereby that rankled after twenty years, a man of whom I have heard it said 'He is always afraid that he is doing something wrong, and generally is,' wrote long stories with apparently no other object than that his persons might show one another, through situations of poignant difficulty, the most exquisite tact.

He did not project, like Henley or like Wilde, an image of himself, because, having all his imagination set on making and doing, he had little self-knowledge. He imagined instead new conditions of making and doing; and, in the teeth of those scientific generalisations that cowed my boyhood, I can see some like imagining in every great change, believing that the first flying fish leaped, not because it sought 'adaptation' to the air, but out of horror of the sea.

X

Soon after I began to attend the lectures, a French class was started in the old coach-house for certain young socialists who planned a tour in France, and I joined it and was for a time a model student constantly encouraged by the compliments of the old French mistress. I told my father of the class, and he asked me to get my sisters admitted. I made difficulties and put off speaking of the matter, for I knew that the new and admirable self I was making would turn, under family eyes, into plain rag doll. How could I pretend to be industrious, and even carry dramatization to the point of learning my lessons, when my sisters were there and knew that I was nothing of the kind? But I had no argument I could use and my sisters were admitted. They said nothing unkind, so far as I can remember, but in a week or two I was my old procrastinating idle self and had soon left the class altogether.

My elder sister stayed on and became an embroideress under Miss May Morris, and the hangings round Morris's big bed at Kelmscott House, Oxfordshire, with their verses about lying happily in bed when 'all birds sing in the town of the tree,' were from her needle though not from her design. She worked for the first few months at Kelmscott House, Hammersmith, and in my imagination I cannot always separate what I saw and heard from her report, or indeed from the report of that tribe or guild who looked up to Morris as to some worshipped mediaeval king. He had no need for other people. I doubt if their marriage or death made him sad or glad, and yet no man I have known was so well loved; you saw him producing everywhere organisation and beauty, seeming, almost in the same instant, helpless and triumphant; and people loved him as children are loved. People much in his neighbourhood became gradually occupied with him, or about his affairs, and without any wish on his part, as simple people become occupied with children. I remember a man who was proud and pleased because he had distracted Morris' thoughts from an attack of gout by leading the conversation delicately to the hated name of Milton. He began at Swinburne. 'Oh, Swinburne,' said Morris, 'is a rhetorician; my masters have been Keats and Chaucer for they make pictures.' 'Does not Milton make pictures?'

asked my informant. 'No,' was the answer, 'Dante makes pictures, but Milton, though he had a great earnest mind, expressed himself as a rhetorician.' 'Great earnest mind,' sounded strange to me and I doubt not that were his questioner not a simple man, Morris had been more violent. Another day the same man started by praising Chaucer, but the gout was worse and Morris cursed Chaucer for destroying the English language with foreign words.

He had few detachable phrases and I can remember little of his speech, which many thought the best of all good talk, except that it matched his burly body and seemed within definite boundaries inexhaustible in fact and expression. He alone of all the men I have known seemed guided by some beast-like instinct and never ate strange meat. 'Balzac! Balzac!' he said to me once, 'Oh, that was the man the French bourgeoisie read so much a few years ago.' I can remember him at supper praising wine: 'Why do people say it is prosaic to be inspired by wine? Has it not been made by the sunlight and the sap?' and his dispraising houses decorated by himself: 'Do you suppose I like that kind of house? I would like a house like a big barn, where one ate in one corner, cooked in another corner, slept in the third corner & in the fourth received one's friends'; and his complaining

44

of Ruskin's objection to the underground railway: 'If you must have a railway the best thing you can do with it is to put it in a tube with a cork at each end.' I remember too that when I asked what led up to his movement, he replied, 'Oh, Ruskin and Carlyle, but somebody should have been beside Carlyle and punched his head every five minutes.' Though I remember little, I do not doubt that, had I continued going there on Sunday evenings, I should have caught fire from his words and turned my hand to some mediaeval work or other. Just before I had ceased to go there I had sent my 'Wanderings of Usheen' to his daughter, hoping of course that it might meet his eyes, & soon after sending it I came upon him by chance in Holborn. 'You write my sort of poetry,' he said and began to praise me and to promise to send his praise to 'The Commonwealth,' the League organ, and he would have said more of a certainty had he not caught sight of a new ornamental cast-iron lamp-post and got very heated upon that subject.

I did not read economics, having turned socialist because of Morris's lectures and pamphlets, and I think it unlikely that Morris himself could read economics. That old dogma of mine seemed germane to the matter. If the men and women imagined by the poets were the norm, and if Morris had, in, let us say, 'News from Nowhere,' then running through 'The Commonwealth,' described such men and women living under their natural conditions or as they would desire to live, then those conditions themselves must be the norm, and could we but get rid of certain institutions the world would turn from eccentricity. Perhaps Morris himself justified himself in his own heart by as simple an argument, and was, as the socialist D... said to me one night walking home after some lecture, 'an anarchist without knowing it.' Certainly I and all about me, including D... himself, were for chopping up the old king for Medea's pot. Morris had told us to have nothing to do with the parliamentary socialists, represented for men in general by the Fabian Society and Hyndman's Socialist Democratic Federation and for us in particular by D... During the period of transition mistakes must be made, and the discredit of these mistakes must be left to 'the bourgeoisie;' and besides, when you begin to talk of this measure or that other you lose sight of the goal and see, to reverse Swinburne's description of Tiresias, 'light on the way but darkness on the goal.' By mistakes Morris meant vexatious restrictions and compromises—'If any man puts me into a labour squad, I will lie on my back and kick.' That phrase very much expresses our idea of revolutionary tactics: we all intended to lie upon our back and kick. D..., pale and sedentary, did not dislike labour squads and we all hated him with the left side of our heads, while admiring him immensely with the right. He alone was invited to entertain Mrs. Morris, having many tales of his Irish uncles, more especially of one particular uncle who had tried to commit suicide by shutting his head into a carpet bag. At that time he was an obscure man, known only for a witty speaker at street corners and in Park demonstrations. He had, with an assumed truculence and fury, cold logic, an universal gentleness, an unruffled courtesy, and yet could never close a speech without being denounced by a journeyman hatter with an Italian name. Converted to socialism by D..., and to anarchism by himself, with swinging arm and uplifted voice this man perhaps exaggerated our scruple about parliament. 'I lack,' said D..., 'the bump of reverence;' whereon the wild man shouted 'You 'ave a 'ole.' There are moments when looking back I somewhat confuse my own figure with that of the hatter, image of our hysteria, for I too became violent with the violent solemnity of a religious devotee. I can even remember sitting behind D... and saying some rude thing or other over his shoulder. I don't remember why I gave it up but I did quite suddenly; and I think the push may have come from a young workman who was educating himself between Morris and Karl Marx. He had planned a history of the navy and when I had spoken of the battleship of Nelson's day, had said: 'Oh, that was the decadence of the battleship,' but if his naval interests were mediaeval, his ideas about religion were pure Karl Marx, and we were soon in perpetual argument. Then gradually the attitude towards religion of almost everybody but Morris, who avoided the subject altogether, got upon my nerves, for I broke out after some lecture or other with all the arrogance of raging youth. They attacked religion, I said, or some such words, and yet there must be a change of heart and only religion could make it. What was the use of talking about some near revolution putting all things right, when the change must come, if come it did, with astronomical slowness, like the cooling of the sun or, it may have been, like the drying of the moon? Morris rang his chairman's bell, but I was too angry to listen, and he had to ring it a second time before I sat down. He said that night at supper: 'Of course I know there must be a change of heart, but it will not come as slowly as all that. I rang my bell because you were not being understood.' He did not show any vexation, but I never returned after that night; and yet I did not always believe what I had said and only gradually gave up thinking of and planning for some near sudden change for the better.

XI

I spent my days at the British Museum and must, I think, have been delicate, for I remember often putting off hour after hour consulting some necessary book because I shrank from lifting the heavy volumes of the catalogue; and yet to save money for my afternoon coffee and roll I often walked the whole way home to Bedford Park. I was compiling, for a series of shilling books, an anthology of Irish fairy stories and, for an American publisher, a two volume selection from the Irish novelists that would be somewhat dearer. I was not well paid, for each book cost me more than three months' reading; and I was paid for the first some twelve pounds, ('O Mr. E...' said publisher to editor, 'you must never again pay so much') and for the second, twenty; but I did not think myself badly paid, for I had chosen the work for my own purposes.

Though I went to Sligo every summer, I was compelled to live out of Ireland the greater part of every year and was but keeping my mind upon what I knew must be the subject matter of my poetry. I believed that if Morris had set his stories amid the scenery of his own Wales (for I knew him to be of Welsh extraction and supposed wrongly that he had spent his childhood there) that if Shelley had nailed his Prometheus or some equal symbol upon some Welsh or Scottish rock, their art had entered more intimately, more microscopically, as it were, into our thought, and had given perhaps to modern poetry a breadth and stability like that of ancient poetry. The statues of Mausolus and Artemisia at the British Museum, private, half animal, half divine figures, all unlike the Grecian athletes and Egyptian kings in their near neighbourhood, that stand in the middle of the crowd's applause or sit above measuring it out unpersuadable justice, became to me, now or later, images of an unpremeditated joyous energy, that neither I nor any other man, racked by doubt and enquiry, can achieve; and that yet, if once achieved, might seem to men and women of Connemara or of Galway their very soul. In our study of that ruined tomb, raised by a queen to her dead lover, and finished by the unpaid labour of great sculptors after her death from grief, or so runs the tale, we cannot distinguish the handiworks of Scopas and Praxiteles; and I wanted to create once more an art, where the artist's handiwork would hide as under those half anonymous chisels, or as we find it in some old Scots ballads or in some twelfth or thirteenth century Arthurian romance. That handiwork assured, I had martyred no man for modelling his own image upon Pallas Athena's buckler; for I took great pleasure in certain allusions to the singer's life one finds in old romances and ballads, and thought his presence there all the more poignant because we discover it half lost, like portly Chaucer riding behind his Maunciple and his Pardoner. Wolfram von Eschenbach, singing his German Parsival, broke off some description of a famished city to remember that in his own house at home the very mice lacked food, and what old ballad singer was it who claimed to have fought by day in the very battle he sang by night? So masterful indeed was that instinct that when the minstrel knew not who his poet was he must needs make up a man: 'When any stranger asks who is the sweetest of singers, answer with one voice: "A blind man; he dwells upon rocky Chios; his songs shall be the most beautiful for ever."' Elaborate modern psychology sounds egotistical, I thought, when it speaks in the first person, but not those simple emotions which resemble the more, the more powerful they are, everybody's emotion, and I was soon to write many poems where an always personal emotion was woven into a general pattern of myth and symbol. When the Fenian poet says that his heart has grown cold and callous, 'For thy hapless fate, dear Ireland, and sorrows of my own,' he but follows tradition, and if he does not move us deeply, it is because he has no sensuous musical vocabulary that comes at need, without compelling him to sedentary toil and so driving him out from his fellows. I thought to create that sensuous, musical vocabulary, and not for myself only but that I might leave it to later Irish poets, much as a mediaeval Japanese painter left his style as an inheritance to his family, and was careful to use a traditional manner and matter; yet did something altogether different, changed by that toil, impelled by my share in Cain's curse, by all that sterile modern complication, by my 'originality' as the newspapers call it. Morris set out to make a revolution that the persons of his 'Well at the World's End' or his 'Waters of the Wondrous Isles,' always, to my mind, in the likeness of Artemisia and her man, might walk his native scenery; and I, that my native scenery might find imaginary inhabitants, half planned a new method and a new culture. My mind began drifting vaguely towards that doctrine of 'the mask' which has convinced me that every passionate man (I have nothing to do with mechanist, or philanthropist, or man whose eyes have no preference) is, as it were, linked with another age, historical or imaginary, where alone he finds images that rouse his energy. Napoleon was never of his own time, as the naturalistic writers and painters bid all men be, but had some Roman Emperor's image in his head and some condottiere's blood in his heart; and when he crowned that head at Rome with his own hands, he had covered, as may be seen from David's painting, his hesitation with that Emperor's old suit.

XII

I had various women friends on whom I would call towards five o'clock, mainly to discuss my thoughts that I could not bring to a man without meeting some competing thought, but partly because their tea & toast saved my pennies for the 'bus ride home; but with women, apart from their intimate exchanges of thought, I was timid and abashed. I was sitting on a seat in front of the British Museum feeding pigeons, when a couple of girls sat near and began enticing my pigeons away, laughing and whispering to one another, and I looked straight in front of me, very indignant, and presently went into the Museum without turning my head towards them. Since then I have often wondered if they were pretty or merely very young. Sometimes I told myself very adventurous love stories with myself for hero, and at other times I planned out a life of lonely austerity, and at other times mixed the ideals and planned a life of lonely austerity mitigated by periodical lapses. I had still the ambition, formed in Sligo in my teens, of living in imitation of Thoreau on Innisfree, a little island in Lough Gill, and when walking through Fleet Street very homesick I heard a little tinkle of water and saw a fountain in a shop window which balanced a little ball upon its jet and began to remember lake water. From the sudden remembrance came my poem 'Innisfree,' my first lyric with anything in its rhythm of my own music. I had begun to loosen rhythm as an escape from rhetoric, and from that emotion of the crowd that rhetoric brings, but I only understood vaguely and occasionally that I must, for my special purpose, use nothing but the common syntax. A couple of years later I would not have written that first line with its conventional archaism—'Arise and go'—nor the inversion in the last stanza. Passing another day by the new Law Courts, a building that I admired because it was Gothic,—'It is not very good,' Morris had said, 'but it is better than any thing else they have got and so they hate it.'—I grew suddenly oppressed by the great weight of stone, and thought, 'There are miles and miles of stone and brick all round me,' and presently added, 'If John the Baptist, or his like, were to come again and had his mind set upon it, he could make all these people go out into some wilderness leaving their buildings empty,' and that thought, which does not seem very valuable now, so enlightened the day that it is still vivid in the memory. I spent a few days at Oxford copying out a seventeenth century translation of *Poggio's Liber Facetiarum* or the *Hypneroto-machia* of *Poliphili* for a publisher; I forget which, for I copied both; and returned very pale to my troubled family. I had lived upon bread and tea because I thought that if antiquity found locust and wild honey nutritive, my soul was strong enough to need no better. I was always planning some great gesture, putting the whole world into one scale of the balance and my soul into the other, and imagining that the whole world somehow kicked the beam. More than thirty years have passed and I have seen no forcible young man of letters brave the metropolis without some like stimulant; and all, after two or three, or twelve or fifteen years, according to obstinacy, have understood that we achieve, if we do achieve, in little diligent sedentary stitches as though we were making lace. I had one unmeasured advantage from my stimulant: I could ink my socks, that they might not show through my shoes, with a most haughty mind, imagining myself, and my torn tackle, somewhere else, in some far place 'under the canopy ... i' the city of kites and crows.'

56

In London I saw nothing good, and constantly remembered that Ruskin had said to some friend of my father's—'As I go to my work at the British Museum I see the faces of the people become daily more corrupt.' I convinced myself for a time, that on the same journey I saw but what he saw. Certain old women's faces filled me with horror, faces that are no longer there, or if they are, pass before me unnoticed: the fat blotched faces, rising above double chins, of women who have drunk too much beer and eaten too much meat. In Dublin I had often seen old women walking with erect heads and gaunt bodies, talking to themselves in loud voices, mad with drink and poverty, but they were different, they belonged to romance: Da Vinci has drawn women who looked so and so carried their bodies.

XIII

I attempted to restore one old friend of my father's to the practice of his youth, but failed though he, unlike my father, had not changed his belief. My father brought me to dine with Jack Nettleship at Wigmore Street, once inventor of imaginative designs and now a painter of melodramatic lions. At dinner I had talked a great deal—too much, I imagine, for so young a man, or may be for any man—and on the way home my father, who had been plainly anxious that I should make a good impression, was very angry. He said I had talked for effect and that talking for effect was precisely what one must never do; he had always hated rhetoric and emphasis and had made me hate it; and his anger plunged me into great dejection. I called at Nettleship's studio the next day to apologise and Nettleship opened the door himself and received me with enthusiasm. He had explained to some woman guest that I would probably talk well, being an Irishman, but the reality had surpassed, etc., etc. I was not flattered, though relieved at not having to apologise, for I soon discovered that what he really admired was my volubility, for he himself was very silent. He seemed about sixty, had a bald head, a grey beard, and a nose, as one of my father's friends used to say, like an opera glass, and sipped cocoa all the afternoon and evening from an enormous tea cup that must have been designed for him alone, not caring how cold the cocoa grew. Years before he had been thrown from his horse while hunting and broken his arm and, because it had been badly set, suffered great pain for along time. A little whiskey would always stop the pain, and soon a little became a great deal and he found himself a drunkard, but having signed his liberty away for certain months he was completely cured. He had acquired, however, the need of some liquid which he could sip constantly. I brought him an admiration settled in early boyhood, for my father had always said, 'George Wilson was our born painter but Nettleship our genius,' and even had he shown me nothing I could care for, I had admired him still because my admiration was in my bones. He showed me his early designs and they, though often badly drawn, fulfilled my hopes. Something of Blake they certainly did show, but had in place of Blake's joyous intellectual energy a Saturnian passion and melancholy. 'God creating evil' the death- like head with a woman and a tiger coming from the forehead, which Rossetti—or was it Browning?—had described 'as the most sublime design of ancient or modern art' had been lost, but there was another version of the same thought and other designs never published or exhibited. They rise before me even now in meditation, especially a blind Titan-like ghost floating with groping hands above the treetops. I wrote a criticism, and arranged for reproductions with the editor of an art magazine, but after it was written and accepted the proprietor, lifting what I considered an obsequious caw in the Huxley, Tyndall, Carolus Duran, Bastien-Lepage rookery, insisted upon its rejection. Nettleship did not mind its rejection, saying, 'Who cares for such things now? Not ten people,' but he did mind my refusal to show him what I had written. Though what I had written was all eulogy, I dreaded his judgment for it was my first art criticism. I hated his big lion pictures, where he attempted an art too much concerned with the sense of touch, with the softness or roughness, the minutely observed irregularity of surfaces, for his genius; and I think he knew it. 'Rossetti used to call my pictures 'pot- boilers,' he said, 'but they are all—all,' and he waved his arms to the canvases, 'symbols.'

60

When I wanted him to design gods and angels and lost spirits once more, he always came back to the point, 'Nobody would be pleased.' 'Everybody should have a *raison d'etre*' was one of his phrases. 'Mrs—'s articles are not good but they are her *raison d'etre.*' I had but little knowledge of art, for there was little scholarship in the Dublin Art School, so I overrated the quality of anything that could be connected with my general beliefs about the world. If I had been able to give angelical, or diabolical names to his lions I might have liked them also and I think that Nettleship himself would have liked them better, and liking them better have become a better painter. We had the same kind of religious feeling, but I could give a crude philosophical expression to mine while he could only express his in action or with brush and pencil. He often told me of certain ascetic ambitions, very much like my own, for he had kept all the moral ambition of youth with a moral courage peculiar to himself, as for instance—'Yeats, the other night I was arrested by a policeman—was walking round Regent's Park barefooted to keep the flesh under—good sort of thing to do—I was carrying my boots in my hand and he thought I was a burglar; and even when I explained and gave him half a crown, he would not let me go till I had promised to put on my boots before I met the next policeman.'

He was very proud and shy, and I could not imagine anybody asking him questions, and so I was content to take these stories as they came, confirmations of stories I had heard in boyhood. One story in particular had stirred my imagination, for, ashamed all my boyhood of my lack of physical courage, I admired what was beyond my imitation. He thought that any weakness, even a weakness of body, had the character of sin, and while at breakfast with his brother, with whom he shared a room on the third floor of a corner house, he said that his nerves were out of order. Presently he left the table, and got out through the window and on to a stone ledge that ran along the wall under the windowsills. He sidled along the ledge, and turning the corner with it, got in at a different window and returned to the table. 'My nerves,' he said, 'are better than I thought.'

XIV

Nettleship said to me: 'Has Edwin Ellis ever said anything about the effect of drink upon my genius?' 'No,' I answered. 'I ask,' he said, 'because I have always thought that Ellis has some strange medical insight.' Though I had answered 'no,' Ellis had only a few days before used these words: 'Nettleship drank his genius away.' Ellis, but lately returned from Perugia, where he had lived many years, was another old friend of my father's but some years younger than Nettleship or my father. Nettleship had found his simplifying image, but in his painting had turned away from it, while Ellis, the son of Alexander Ellis, a once famous man of science, who was perhaps the last man in England to run the circle of the sciences without superficiality, had never found that image at all. He was a painter and poet, but his painting, which did not interest me, showed no influence but that of Leighton. He had started

63

perhaps a couple of years too late for Pre-Raphaelite influence, for no great Pre-Raphaelite picture
was painted after 1870, and left England too soon
for that of the French painters. He was, however,
sometimes moving as a poet and still more often
an astonishment. I have known him cast something just said into a dozen lines of musical verse,
without apparently ceasing to talk; but the work
once done he could not or would not amend it,
and my father thought he lacked all ambition. Yet
he had at times nobility of rhythm—an instinct
for grandeur—and after thirty years I still repeat
to myself his address to Mother Earth:

> *O mother of the hills, forgive our towers;*
> *O mother of the clouds, forgive our dreams*

and there are certain whole poems that I read from
time to time or try to make others read. There is
that poem where the manner is unworthy of the
matter, being loose and facile, describing Adam
and Eve fleeing from Paradise. Adam asks Eve
what she carries so carefully and Eve replies that
it is a little of the apple core kept for their children. There is that vision of 'Christ the Less,' a
too hurriedly written ballad, where the half of
Christ, sacrificed to the divine half 'that fled to
seek felicity,' wanders wailing through Golgotha;
and there is 'The Saint and the Youth' in which

I can discover no fault at all. He loved complexities—'seven silences like candles round her face' is a line of his—and whether he wrote well or ill had always a manner, which I would have known from that of any other poet. He would say to me, 'I am a mathematician with the mathematics left out'—his father was a great mathematician—or 'A woman once said to me, "Mr. Ellis why are your poems like sums?"' and certainly he loved symbols and abstractions. He said once, when I had asked him not to mention something or other, 'Surely you have discovered by this time that I know of no means whereby I can mention a fact in conversation.'

He had a passion for Blake, picked up in Pre-Raphaelite studios, and early in our acquaintance put into my hands a scrap of note paper on which he had written some years before an interpretation of the poem that begins

The fields from Islington to Marylebone
To Primrose Hill and St. John's Wood
Were builded over with pillars of gold
And there Jerusalem's pillars stood.

The four quarters of London represented Blake's four great mythological personages, the Zoas, and also the four elements. These few sentences were the foundation of all study of the philosophy of William Blake, that requires an exact knowledge for its pursuit and that traces the connection between his system and that of Swedenborg or of Boehme. I recognised certain attributions, from what is sometimes called the Christian Cabala, of which Ellis had never heard, and with this proof that his interpretation was more than phantasy, he and I began our four years' work upon the Prophetic Books of William Blake. We took it as almost a sign of Blake's personal help when we discovered that the spring of 1889, when we first joined our knowledge, was one hundred years from the publication of 'The Book of Thel,' the first published of the Prophetic Books, as though it were firmly established that the dead delight in anniversaries. After months of discussion and reading, we made a concordance of all Blake's mystical terms, and there was much copying to be done in the Museum & at Red Hill, where the descendants of Blake's friend and patron, the landscape painter, John Linnell, had many manuscripts. The Linnellswere narrow in their religious ideas & doubtful of Blake's orthodoxy, whom they held, however, in great honour, and I remember a timid old lady who had known Blake when a child saying: 'He had very wrong ideas, he did not believe in the historical Jesus.' One old man sat always beside us ostensibly to sharpen our pencils, but perhaps really to see that we did not steal the manuscripts, and they gave us very old port at lunch and I have upon my dining room walls their present of Blake's Dante engravings. Going thither and returning Ellis would entertain me by philosophical discussion, varied with improvised stories, at first folk tales which he professed to have picked up in Scotland; and though I had read and collected many folk tales, I did not see through the deceit. I have a partial memory of two more elaborate tales, one of an Italian conspirator flying barefoot from I forget what adventure through I forget what Italian city, in the early morning. Fearing to be recognised by his bare feet, he slipped past the sleepy porter at an hotel calling out 'number so and so' as if he were some belated guest. Then passing from bedroom door to door he tried on the boots, and just as he got a pair to fit a voice cried from the room 'Who is that?' 'Merely me, sir,' he called back, 'taking your boots.' The other was of a Martyr's Bible round which the cardinal virtues had taken personal form—this a fragment of Blake's philosophy. It was in the possession of an old clergyman when a certain jockey called upon him, and the cardinal virtues, confused between jockey and clergyman, devoted themselves to the jockey. As whenever he sinned a cardinal virtue interfered and turned him back to virtue, he lived in great credit and

67

made, but for one sentence, a very holy death. As his wife and family knelt round in admiration and grief, he suddenly said 'Damn.' 'O my dear,' said his wife, 'what a dreadful expression.' He answered, 'I am going to heaven' and straightway died. It was a long tale, for there were all the jockey's vain attempts to sin, as well as all the adventures of the clergyman, who became very sinful indeed, but it ended happily, for when the jockey died the cardinal virtues returned to the clergyman. I think he would talk to any audience that offered, one audience being the same as another in his eyes, and it may have been for this reason that my father called him unambitious. When he was a young man he had befriended a reformed thief and had asked the grateful thief to take him round the thieves' quarters of London. The thief, however, hurried him away from the worst saying, 'Another minute and they would have found you out. If they were not the stupidest men in London, they had done so already.' Ellis had gone through a no doubt romantic and witty account of all the houses he had robbed, and all the throats he had cut in one short life.

His conversation would often pass out of my comprehension, or indeed I think of any man's, into a labyrinth of abstraction and subtilty, and then suddenly return with some verbal conceit or turn of wit. The mind is known to attain, in certain conditions of trance, a quickness so extraordinary that we are compelled at times to imagine a condition of unendurable intellectual intensity, from which we are saved by the merciful stupidity of the body; & I think that the mind of Edwin Ellis was constantly upon the edge of trance. Once we were discussing the symbolism of sex, in the philosophy of Blake, and had been in disagreement all the afternoon. I began talking with a new sense of conviction, and after a moment Ellis, who was at his easel, threw down his brush and said that he had just seen the same explanation in a series of symbolic visions. 'In another moment,' he said, 'I should have been off.' We went into the open air and walked up and down to get rid of that feeling, but presently we came in again and I began again my explanation, Ellis lying upon the sofa. I had been talking some time when Mrs. Ellis came into the room and said: 'Why are you sitting in the dark?' Ellis answered, 'But we are not,' and then added in a voice of wonder, 'I thought the lamp was lit and that I was sitting up, and I find I am in the dark and lying down.' I had seen a flicker of light over the ceiling, but had thought it a reflection from some light outside the house, which may have been the case.

XV

I had already met most of the poets of my generation. I had said, soon after the publication of 'The Wanderings of Usheen,' to the editor of a series of shilling reprints, who had set me to compile tales of the Irish fairies, 'I am growing jealous of other poets, and we will all grow jealous of each other unless we know each other and so feel a share in each other's triumph.' He was a Welshman, lately a mining engineer, Ernest Rhys, a writer of Welsh translations and original poems that have often moved me greatly though I can think of no one else who has read them. He was seven or eight years older than myself and through his work as editor knew everybody who would compile a book for seven or eight pounds. Between us we founded 'The Rhymers' Club' which for some years was to meet every night in an upper room with a sanded floor in an ancient eating house in the Strand called 'The Cheshire Cheese.'

Lionel Johnson, Ernest Dowson, Victor Plarr, Ernest Radford, John Davidson, Richard le Gallienne, T. W. Rolleston, Selwyn Image and two men of an older generation, Edwin Ellis and John Todhunter, came constantly for a time, Arthur Symons and Herbert Home less constantly, while William Watson joined but never came and Francis Thompson came once but never joined; and sometimes, if we met in a private house, which we did occasionally, Oscar Wilde came. It had been useless to invite him to the 'Cheshire Cheese' for he hated Bohemia. 'Olive Schreiner,' he said once to me, 'is staying in the East End because that is the only place where people do not wear masks upon their faces, but I have told her that I live in the West End because nothing in life interests me but the mask.'

We read our poems to one another and talked criticism and drank a little wine. I sometimes say when I speak of the club, 'We had such and such ideas, such and such a quarrel with the great Victorians, we set before us such and such aims,' as though we had many philosophical ideas. I say this because I am ashamed to admit that I had these ideas and that whenever I began to talk of them a gloomy silence fell upon the room. A young Irish poet, who wrote excellently but had the worst manners, was to say a few years later,

'You do not talk like a poet, you talk like a man of letters;' and if all the rhymers had not been polite, if most of them had not been to Oxford or Cambridge, they would have said the same thing. I was full of thought, often very abstract thought, longing all the while to be full of images, because I had gone to the art school instead of a university. Yet even if I had gone to a university, and learned all the classical foundations of English literature and English culture, all that great erudition which, once accepted, frees the mind from restlessness, I should have had to give up my Irish subject matter, or attempt to found a new tradition. Lacking sufficient recognised precedent I must needs find out some reason for all I did. I knew almost from the start that to overflow with reasons was to be not quite well-born, and when I could I hid them, as men hide a disagreeable ancestry; and that there was no help for it, seeing that my country was not born at all. I was of those doomed to imperfect achievement, and under a curse, as it were, like some race of birds compelled to spend the time, needed for the making of the nest, in argument as to the convenience of moss and twig and lichen. Le Gallienne and Davidson, and even Symons, were provincial at their setting out, but their provincialism was curable, mine incurable; while the one conviction shared by all the younger men, but principally by Johnson and

Horne, who imposed their personalities upon us, was an opposition to all ideas, all generalisations that can be explained and debated. E... fresh from Paris would sometimes say—'We are concerned with nothing but impressions,' but that itself was a generalisation and met but stony silence. Conversation constantly dwindled into 'Do you like so and so's last book?' 'No, I prefer the book before it,' and I think that but for its Irish members, who said whatever came into their heads, the club would not have survived its first difficult months. I knew—now ashamed that I thought 'like a man of letters,' now exasperated at their indifference to the fashion of their own river bed—that Swinburne in one way, Browning in another, and Tennyson in a third, had filled their work with what I called 'impurities,' curiosities about politics, about science, about history, about religion; and that we must create once more the pure work.

Our clothes were for the most part unadventurous like our conversation, though I indeed wore a brown velveteen coat, a loose tie and a very old Inverness cape, discarded by my father twenty years before and preserved by my Sligo-born mother whose actions were unreasoning and habitual like the seasons. But no other member of the club, except Le Gallienne, who wore a loose tie, and Symons, who had an Inverness cape that was quite new & almost fashionable, would have shown himself for the world in any costume but 'that of an English gentleman.' 'One should be quite unnoticeable,' Johnson explained to me. Those who conformed most carefully to the fashion in their clothes generally departed furthest from it in their hand-writing, which was small, neat and studied, one poet—which I forget—having founded his upon the handwriting of George Herbert. Dowson and Symons I was to know better in later years when Symons became a very dear friend, and I never got behind John Davidson's Scottish roughness and exasperation, though I saw much of him, but from the first I devoted myself to Lionel Johnson. He and Horne and Image and one or two others shared a man-servant and an old house in Charlotte Street, Fitzroy Square, typical figures of transition, doing as an achievement of learning and of exquisite taste what their predecessors did in careless abundance. All were Pre-Raphaelite, and sometimes one might meet in the rooms of one or other a ragged figure, as of some fallen dynasty, Simeon Solomon, the Pre- Raphaelite painter, once the friend of Rossetti and of Swinburne, but fresh now from some low public house. Condemned to a long term of imprisonment for a criminal offence, he had sunk into drunkenness and misery. Introduced one night, however, to some man who mistook him, in the dim candle light, for another Solomon, a successful academic painter and R. A., he started to his feet in a rage with 'Sir, do you dare to mistake me for that mountebank?' Though not one had harkened to the feeblest caw, or been spattered by the smallest dropping from any Huxley, Tyndall, Carolus Duran, Bastien-Lepage bundle of old twigs, I began by suspecting them of lukewarmness, and even backsliding, and I owe it to that suspicion that I never became intimate with Horne, who lived to become the greatest English authority upon Italian life in the fourteenth century and to write the one standard work on Botticelli. Connoisseur in several arts, he had designed a little church in the manner of Inigo Jones for a burial ground near the Marble Arch. Though I now think his little church a masterpiece, its style was more than a century too late to hit my fancy at two or three and twenty; and I accused him of leaning towards that eighteenth century

> *That taught a school*
> *Of dolts to smooth, inlay, and clip, and fit*
> *Till, like the certain wands of Jacob's wit,*
> *Their verses tallied.*

Another fanaticism delayed my friendship with two men, who are now my friends and in certain matters my chief instructors. Somebody, probably

Lionel Johnson, brought me to the studio of Charles Ricketts and Charles Shannon, certainly heirs of the great generation, and the first thing I saw was a Shannon picture of a lady and child arrayed in lace, silk and satin, suggesting that hated century. My eyes were full of some more mythological mother and child and I would have none of it, and I told Shannon that he had not painted a mother and child but elegant people expecting visitors and I thought that a great reproach. Somebody writing in 'The Germ' had said that a picture of a pheasant and an apple was merely a picture of something to eat, and I was so angry with the indifference to subject, which was the commonplace of all art criticism since Bastien-Lepage, that I could at times see nothing else but subject. I thought that, though it might not matter to the man himself whether he loved a white woman or a black, a female pickpocket or a regular communicant of the Church of England, if only he loved strongly, it certainly did matter to his relations and even under some circumstances to his whole neighbourhood. Sometimes indeed, like some father in Moliere, I ignored the lover's feelings altogether and even refused to admit that a trace of the devil, perhaps a trace of colour, may lend piquancy, especially if the connection be not permanent.

Among these men, of whom so many of the greatest talents were to live such passionate lives and die such tragic deaths, one serene man, T. W. Rolleston, seemed always out of place. It was I brought him there, intending to set him to some work in Ireland later on. I have known young Dublin working men slip out of their workshop to see 'the second Thomas Davis' passing by, and even remember a conspiracy, by some three or four, to make him 'the leader of the Irish race at home & abroad,' and all because he had regular features; and when all is said, Alexander the Great & Alcibiades were personable men, and the Founder of the Christian religion was the only man who was neither a little too tall nor a little too short but exactly six feet high. We in Ireland thought as do the plays and ballads, not understanding that, from the first moment wherein nature foresaw the birth of Bastien-Lepage, she has only granted great creative power to men whose faces are contorted with extravagance or curiosity or dulled with some protecting stupidity.

I had now met all those who were to make the nineties of the last century tragic in the history of literature, but as yet we were all seemingly equal, whether in talent or in luck, and scarce even personalities to one another. I remember saying one night at the Cheshire Cheese, when more poets than usual had come, 'None of us can say who will succeed, or even who has or has not talent. The only thing certain about us is that we are too many.'

XVI

I have described what image—always opposite to the natural self or the natural world—Wilde, Henley, Morris copied or tried to copy, but I have not said if I found an image for myself. I know very little about myself and much less of that anti-self: probably the woman who cooks my dinner or the woman who sweeps out my study knows more than I. It is perhaps because nature made me a gregarious man, going hither and thither looking for conversation, and ready to deny from fear or favour his dearest conviction, that I love proud and lonely images. When I was a child and went daily to the sexton's daughter for writing lessons, I found one poem in her School Reader that delighted me beyond all others: a fragment of some metrical translation from Aristophanes wherein the birds sing scorn upon mankind. In later years my mind gave itself to gregarious Shelley's dream of a young man, his hair blanched with sorrow studying philosophy in some lonely tower, or of his old man, master of all human knowledge, hidden from human sight in some shell-strewn cavern on the Mediterranean shore. One passage above all ran perpetually in my ears—

Some feign that he is Enoch: others dream
He was pre-Adamite, and has survived
Cycles of generation and of ruin.
The sage, in truth, by dreadful abstinence,
And conquering penance of the mutinous flesh, Deep
contemplation and unwearied study,
In years outstretched beyond the date of man,
May have attained to sovereignty and science
Over those strong and secret things and thoughts
Which others fear and know not.

MAHMUD

I would talk
With this old Jew.

HASSAN

Thy will is even now
Made known to him where he dwells in a sea-cavern
'Mid the Demonesi, less accessible
Than thou or God! He who would question him
Must sail alone at sunset where the stream
Of ocean sleeps around those foamless isles, When the
young moon is westering as now,

And evening airs wander upon the wave;
And, when the pines of that bee-pasturing isle,
Green Erebinthus, quench the fiery shadow
Of his gilt prow within the sapphire water,
Then must the lonely helmsman cry aloud
'Ahasuerus!' and the caverns round
Will answer 'Ahasuerus!' If his prayer
Be granted, a faint meteor will arise,
Lighting him over Marmora; and a wind
Will rush out of the sighing pine-forest,
And with the wind a storm of harmony
Unutterably sweet, and pilot him
Through the soft twilight to the Bosphorus:
Thence, at the hour and place and circumstance
Fit for the matter of their conference,
The Jew appears. Few dare, and few who dare
Win the desired communion.

Already in Dublin, I had been attracted to the Theosophists because they had affirmed the real existence of the Jew, or of his like; and, apart from whatever might have been imagined by Huxley, Tyndall, Carolus Duran and Bastien-Lepage, I saw nothing against his reality. Presently having heard that Madame Blavatsky had arrived from France, or from India, I thought it time to look the matter up. Certainly if wisdom existed anywhere in the world it must be in some such lonely mind admitting no duty to us, communing with

God only, conceding nothing from fear or favour. Have not all peoples, while bound together in a single mind and taste, believed that such men existed and paid them that honour, or paid it to their mere shadow, which they have refused to philanthropists and to men of learning?

I found Madame Blavatsky in a little house at Norwood, with but, as she said, three followers left—the Society of Psychical Research had just reported on her Indian phenomena—and as one of the three followers sat in an outer room to keep out undesirable visitors, I was kept a long time kicking my heels. Presently I was admitted and found an old woman in a plain loose dark dress: a sort of old Irish peasant woman with an air of humour and audacious power. I was still kept waiting, for she was deep in conversation with a woman visitor. I strayed through folding doors into the next room and stood, in sheer idleness of mind, looking at a cuckoo clock. It was certainly stopped, for the weights were off and lying upon the ground, and yet as I stood there the cuckoo came out and cuckooed at me. I interrupted Madame Blavatsky to say. 'Your clock has hooted me.' 'It often hoots at a stranger,' she replied. 'Is there a spirit in it?' I said. 'I do not know,' she said, 'I should have to be alone to know what is in it.' I went back to the clock and began examining it and heard her say 'Do not break my clock.' I wondered if there was some hidden mechanism, and I should have been put out, I suppose, had I found any, though Henley had said to me, 'Of course she gets up fraudulent miracles, but a person of genius has to do something; Sarah Bernhardt sleeps in her coffin.' Presently the visitor went away and Madame Blavatsky explained that she was a propagandist for women's rights who had called to find out 'why men were so bad.' 'What explanation did you give her?' I said. 'That men were born bad but women made themselves so,' and then she explained that I had been kept waiting because she had mistaken me for some man whose name resembled mine and who wanted to persuade her of the flatness of the earth.

When I next saw her she had moved into a house at Holland Park, and some time must have passed— probably I had been in Sligo where I returned constantly for long visits—for she was surrounded by followers. She sat nightly before a little table covered with green baize and on this green baize she scribbled constantly with a piece of white chalk. She would scribble symbols, sometimes humorously applied, and sometimes unintelligible figures, but the chalk was intended to mark down her score when she played patience. One saw in the next room a large table where every night her followers and guests, often a great number, sat down to their vegetarian meal, while she encouraged or mocked through the folding doors. A great passionate nature, a sort of female Dr. Johnson, impressive, I think, to every man or woman who had themselves any richness, she seemed impatient of the formalism, of the shrill abstract idealism of those about her, and this impatience broke out inrailing & many nicknames: 'O you are a flapdoodle, but then you are a theosophist and a brother. 'The most devout and learned of all her followers said to me, 'H.P.B. has just told me that there is another globe stuck on to this at the north pole, so that the earth has really a shape something like a dumb-bell.' I said, for I knew that her imagination contained all the folklore of the world, 'That must be some piece of Eastern mythology.' 'O no it is not,' he said, 'of that I am certain, and there must be something in it or she would not have said it.' Her mockery was not kept for her followers alone, and her voice would become harsh, and her mockery lose phantasy and humour, when she spoke of what seemed to her scientific materialism. Once I saw this antagonism, guided by some kind of telepathic divination, take a form of brutal phantasy. I brought a very able Dublin woman to see her and this woman had a brother, a physiologist whose reputation, though known to specialists alone, was European; and, because of this brother, a family pride in everything scientific and modern. The Dublin woman scarcely opened her mouth the whole evening and her name was certainly unknown to Madame Blavatsky, yet I saw at once in that wrinkled old face bent over the cards, and the only time I ever saw it there, a personal hostility, the dislike of one woman for another. Madame Blavatsky seemed to bundle herself up, becoming all primeval peasant, and began complaining of her ailments, more especially of her bad leg. But of late her master—her 'old Jew,' her 'Ahasuerus,' cured it, or set it on the way to be cured. 'I was sitting here in my chair,' she said, 'when the master came in and brought something with him which he put over my knee, something warm which enclosed my knee—it was a live dog which he had cut open.' I recognised a cure used sometimes in mediaeval medicine. She had two masters, and their portraits, ideal Indian heads, painted by some most incompetent artist, stood upon either side of the folding doors. One night, when talk was impersonal and general, I sat gazing through the folding doors into the dimly lighted dining-room beyond. I noticed a curious red light shining upon a picture and got up to see where the red light came from. It was the picture of an Indian and as I came near it slowly vanished. When I returned to my seat, Madame Blavatsky said, 'What did you see?' 'A picture,' I said. 'Tell it to go away.' 'It is already gone.' 'So much the better,' she said, 'I was afraid it was medium ship but it is only clairvoyance.' 'What is the difference?' 'If it had been medium ship, it would have stayed in spite of you. Beware of medium ship; it is a kind of madness; I know, for I have been through it.'

I found her almost always full of gaiety that, unlike the occasional joking of those about her, was illogical and incalculable and yet always kindly and tolerant. I had called one evening to find her absent, but expected every moment. She had been somewhere at the seaside for her health and arrived with a little suite of followers. She sat down at once in her big chair, and began unfolding a brown paper parcel, while all looked on full of curiosity. It contained a large family Bible. 'This is a present for my maid,' she said. 'What! A Bible and not even anointed!' said some shocked voice. 'Well my children,' was the answer, 'what is the good of giving lemons to those who want oranges?' When I first began to frequent her house, as I soon did very constantly, I noticed a handsome clever woman of the world there, who seemed certainly very much out of place, penitent though she thought herself. Presently there was much scandal and gossip, for the penitent was plainly entangled with two young men, who were expected to grow into ascetic sages. The scandal was so great that

Madame Blavatsky had to call the penitent before her and to speak after this fashion, 'We think that it is necessary to crush the animal nature; you should live in chastity in act and thought. Initiation is granted only to those who are entirely chaste,' and so to run on for some time. However, after some minutes in that vehement style, the penitent standing crushed and shamed before her, she had wound up, 'I cannot permit you more than one.' She was quite sincere, but thought that nothing mattered but what happened in the mind, and that if we could not master the mind, our actions were of little importance. One young man filled her with exasperation; for she thought that his settled gloom came from his chastity. I had known him in Dublin, where he had been accustomed to interrupt long periods of asceticism, in which he would eat vegetables and drink water, with brief outbreaks of what he considered the devil. After an outbreak he would for a few hours dazzle the imagination of the members of the local theosophical society with poetical rhapsodies about harlots and street lamps, and then sink into weeks of melancholy. A fellow theosophist once found him hanging from the window pole, but cut him down in the nick of time. I said to the man who cut him down, 'What did you say to one another?' He said, 'We spent the night telling comic stories and laughing a great deal.' This man, torn between sensuality and visionary ambition, was now the most devout of all, and told me that in the middle of the night he could often hear the ringing of the little 'astral bell' whereby Madame Blavatsky's master called her attention, and that, although it was a low silvery sound it made the whole house shake. Another night I found him waiting in the hall to show in those who had the right of entrance on some night when the discussion was private, and as I passed he whispered into my ear, 'Madame Blavatsky is perhaps not a real woman at all. They say that her dead body was found many years ago upon some Russian battlefield.' She had two dominant moods, both of extreme activity, but one calm and philosophic, and this was the mood always on that night in the week, when she answered questions upon her system; and as I look back after thirty years I often ask myself 'Was her speech automatic? Was she for one night, in every week, a trance medium, or in some similar state?' In the other mood she was full of phantasy and inconsequent raillery. 'That is the Greek church, a triangle like all true religion,' I recall her saying, as she chalked out a triangle on the green baize, and then, as she made it disappear in meaningless scribbles 'it spread out and became a bramble-bush like the Church of Rome.' Then rubbing it all out except one straight line, 'Now they have lopped off the branches and turned it into a broomstick arid that is Protestantism.' And so it was, night after night, always varied and unforseen. I have observed a like sudden extreme change in others, half whose thought was supernatural, and Laurence Oliphant records some where or other like observations. I can remember only once finding her in a mood of reverie; something had happened to damp her spirits, some attack upon her movement, or upon herself. She spoke of Balzac, whom she had seen but once, of Alfred de Musset, whom she had known well enough to dislike for his morbidity, and of George Sand whom she had known so well that they had dabbled in magic together of which 'neither knew anything at all' in those days; and she ran on, as if there was nobody there to overhear her, 'I used to wonder at and pity the people who sell their souls to the devil, but now I only pity them. They do it to have somebody on their sides,' and added to that, after some words I have forgotten, 'I write, write, write as the Wandering Jew walks, walks, walks.' Besides the devotees, who came to listen and to turn every doctrine into a new sanction for the puritanical convictions of their Victorian childhood, cranks came from half Europe and from all America, and they came that they might talk. One American said to me, 'She has become the most famous woman in the world by sitting in a big chair and permitting us to talk.' They talked and she played patience, and totted up her score on the green baize, and generally seemed to listen, but sometimes she would listen no more. There was a woman who talked perpetually of 'the divine spark' within her, until Madame Blavatsky stopped her with—'Yes, my dear, you have a divine spark within you, and if you are not very careful you will hear it snore.' A certain Salvation Army captain probably pleased her, for, if vociferous and loud of voice, he had much animation. He had known hardship and spoke of his visions while starving in the streets and he was still perhaps a little light in the head. I wondered what he could preach to ignorant men, his head ablaze with wild mysticism, till I met a man who had heard him talking near Covent Garden to some crowd in the street. 'My friends,' he was saying, 'you have the kingdom of heaven within you and it would take a pretty big pill to get that out.'

XVII

Meanwhile I had not got any nearer to proving that 'Ahasuerus dwells in a sea-cavern 'mid the Demonesi,' but one conclusion I certainly did come to, which I find written out in an old diary and dated 1887. Madame Blavatsky's 'masters' were 'trance' personalities, but by 'trance personalities' I meant something almost as exciting as 'Ahasuerus' himself. Years before I had found, on a table in the Royal Irish Academy, a pamphlet on Japanese art, and read there of an animal painter so remarkable that horses he had painted upon a temple wall had stepped down after and trampled the neighbouring fields of rice. Somebody had come to the temple in the early morning, been startled by a shower of water drops, looked up and seen a painted horse, still wet from the dew-covered fields, but now 'trembling into stillness.' I thought that her masters were imaginary forms created by suggestion, but whether that suggestion came from Madame Blavatsky's own mind or from some mind, perhaps at a great distance, I did not know; and I believed that these forms could pass from Madame Blavatsky's mind to the minds of others, and even acquire external reality, and that it was even possible that they talked and wrote. They were born in the imagination, where Blake had declared that all men live after death, and where 'every man is king or priest in his own house.' Certainly the house at Holland Park was a romantic place, where one heard of constant apparitions and exchanged speculations like those of the middle ages, and I did not separate myself from it by my own will. The Secretary, an intelligent and friendly man, asked me to come and see him, and when I did, complained that I was causing discussion and disturbance, a certain fanatical hungry face had been noticed red and tearful, & it was quite plain that I was not in full agreement with their method or their philosophy. 'I know,' he said, 'that all these people become dogmatic and fanatical because they believe what they can never prove; that their withdrawal from family life is to them a great misfortune; but what are we to do? We have been told that all spiritual influx into the society will come to an end in 1897 for exactly one hundred years. Before that date our fundamental ideas must be spread through the world.'

I knew the doctrine and it had made me wonder why that old woman, or rather 'the trance personalities' who directed her and were her genius, insisted upon it, for influx of some kind there must always be. Did they dread heresy after the death of Madame Blavatsky, or had they no purpose but the greatest possible immediate effort?

XVIII

At the British Museum reading-room I often saw a man of thirty-six or thirty-seven, in a brown velveteen coat, with a gaunt resolute face, and an athletic body, who seemed before I heard his name, or knew the nature of his studies, a figure of romance. Presently I was introduced, where or by what man or woman I do not remember. He was Macgregor Mathers, the author of the 'Kabbalas Unveiled,' & his studies were two only—magic and the theory of war, for he believed himself a born commander and all but equal in wisdom and in power to that old Jew. He had copied many manuscripts on magic ceremonial and doctrine in the British Museum, and was to copy many more in continental libraries, and it was through him mainly that I began certain studies and experiences that were to convince me that images well up before the mind's eye from a deeper source than conscious or subconscious memory. I believe that his mind in those early days did not belie his face and body, though in later years it became unhinged, for he kept a proud head amid great poverty. One that boxed with him nightly has told me that for many weeks he could knock him down, though Macgregor was the stronger man, and only knew long after that during those weeks Macgregor starved. With him I met an old white-haired Oxfordshire clergyman, the most panic-stricken person I have ever known, though Macgregor's introduction had been 'He unites us to the great adepts of antiquity.' This old man took me aside that he might say—'I hope you never invoke spirits—that is a very dangerous thing to do. I am told that even the planetary spirits turn upon us in the end.' I said, 'Have you ever seen an apparition?' 'O yes, once,' he said. 'I have my alchemical laboratory in a cellar under my house where the Bishop cannot see it. One day I was walking up & down there when I heard another footstep walking up and down beside me. I turned and saw a girl I had been in love with when I was a young man, but she died long ago. She wanted me to kiss her. Oh no, I would not do that.' 'Why not?' I said. 'Oh, she might have got power over me.' 'Has your alchemical research had any success?' I said. 'Yes, I once made the elixir of life. A French alchemist said it had the right smell and the right colour,' (The alchemist may have been Elephas Levi, who visited England in the sixties, & would have said anything) 'but the first effect of the elixir is that your nails fall out and your hair falls off. I was afraid that I might have made a mistake and that nothing else might happen, so I put it away on a shelf. I meant to drink it when I was an old man, but when I got it down the other day it had all dried up.'

XIX

I generalized a great deal and was ashamed of it. I thought that it was my business in life to be an artist and a poet, and that there could be no business comparable to that. I refused to read books, and even to meet people who excited me to generalization, but all to no purpose. I said my prayers much as in childhood, though without the old regularity of hour and place, and I began to pray that my imagination might somehow be rescued from abstraction, and become as pre-occupied with life as had been the imagination of Chaucer. For ten or twelve years more I suffered continual remorse, and only became content when my abstractions had composed themselves into picture and dramatization. My very remorse helped to spoil my early poetry, giving it an element of sentimentality through my refusal to permit it any share of an intellect which I considered impure. Even in practical life I only very gradually began to use generalizations, that have since become the foundation of all I have done, or shall do, in Ireland. For all I know, all men may have been as timid; for I am persuaded that our intellects at twenty contain all the truths we shall ever find, but as yet we do not know truths that belong to us from opinions caught up in casual irritation or momentary phantasy. As life goes on we discover that certain thoughts sustain us in defeat, or give us victory, whether over ourselves or others, & it is these thoughts, tested by passion, that we call convictions. Among subjective men (in all those, that is, who must spin a web out of their own bowels) the victory is an intellectual daily recreation of all that exterior fate snatches away, and so that fate's antithesis; while what I have called 'The mask' is an emotional antithesis to all that comes out of their internal nature. We begin to live when we have conceived life as a tragedy.

XX

A conviction that the world was now but a bundle of fragments possessed me without ceasing. I had tried this conviction on 'The Rhymers,' thereby plunging into greater silence an already too silent evening. 'Johnson,' I was accustomed to say, 'you are the only man I know whose silence has beak & claw.' I had lectured on it to some London Irish society, and I was to lecture upon it later on in Dublin, but I never found but one interested man, an official of the Primrose League, who was also an active member of the Fenian Brotherhood. 'I am an extreme conservative apart from Ireland,' I have heard him explain; and I have no doubt that personal experience made him share the sight of any eye that saw the world in fragments. I had been put into a rage by the followers of Huxley, Tyndall, Carolus Duran and Bastien-Lepage, who not only asserted the unimportance of subject, whether in art or literature, but the independence of the arts from one another. Upon the other hand I delighted in every age where poet and artist confined themselves gladly to some inherited subject matter known to the whole people, for I thought that in man and race alike there is something called 'unity of being,' using that term as Dante used it when he compared beauty in the *Convito* to a perfectly proportioned human body. My father, from whom I had learned the term, preferred a comparison to a musical instrument so strong that if we touch a string all the strings murmur faintly. There is not more desire, he had said, in lust than in true love; but in true love desire awakens pity, hope, affection, admiration, and, given appropriate circumstance, every emotion possible to man. When I began, however, to apply this thought to the State and to argue for a law-made balance among trades and occupations, my father displayed at once the violent free-trader and propagandist of liberty. I thought that the enemy of this unity was abstraction, meaning by abstraction not the distinction but the isolation of occupation, or class or faculty—

> 'Call down the hawk from the air
> Let him be hooded, or caged,
> Till the yellow eye has grown mild,
> For larder and spit are bare,
> The old cook enraged,
> The scullion gone wild.'

I knew no mediaeval cathedral, and Westminster, being a part of abhorred London, did not interest me; but I thought constantly of Homer and Dante and the tombs of Mausolus and Artemisa, the great figures of King and Queen and the lesser figures of Greek and Amazon, Centaur and Greek. I thought that all art should be a Centaur finding in the popular lore its back and its strong legs. I got great pleasure too from remembering that Homer was sung, and from that tale of Dante hearing a common man sing some stanza from 'The Divine Comedy,' and from Don Quixote's meeting with some common man that sang Ariosto. Morris had never seemed to care for any poet later than Chaucer; and though I preferred Shakespeare to Chaucer I begrudged my own preference. Had not Europe shared one mind and heart, until both mind and heart began to break into fragments a little before Shakespeare's birth? Music and verse began to fall apart when Chaucer robbed verse of its speed that he might give it greater meditation, though for another generation or so minstrels were to sing his long elaborated 'Troilus and Cressida;' painting parted from religion in the later Renaissance that it might study effects of tangibility undisturbed; while, that it might characterise, where it had once personified, it renounced, in our own age, all that inherited subject matter which we have named poetry.

Presently I was indeed to number character itself among the abstractions, encouraged by Congreve's saying that 'passions are too powerful in the fair sex to let humour,' or as we say character, 'have its course.' Nor have we fared better under the common daylight, for pure reason has notoriously made but light of practical reason, and has been made but light of in its turn, from that morning when Descartes discovered that he could think better in his bed than out of it; nor needed I original thought to discover, being so late of the school of Morris, that machinery had not separated from handicraft wholly for the world's good; nor to notice that the distinction of classes had become their isolation. If the London merchants of our day competed together in writing lyrics they would not, like the Tudor merchants, dance in the open street before the house of the victor; nor do the great ladies of London finish their balls on the pavement before their doors as did the great Venetian ladies even in the eighteenth century, conscious of an all enfolding sympathy. Doubtless because fragments broke into even smaller fragments we saw one another in a light of bitter comedy, and in the arts, where now one technical element reigned and now another, generation hated generation, and accomplished beauty was snatched away when it had most engaged our affections. One thing I did not foresee, not having the courage of my own thought—the growing murderousness of the world.

Turning and turning in the widening gyre
The falcon cannot hear the falconer;
Things fall apart; the centre cannot hold;
Mere anarchy is loosed upon the world,
The blood-dimmed tide is loosed, and everywhere
The ceremony of innocence is drowned;
The best lack all conviction, while the worst
Are full of passionate intensity.

XXI

The Huxley, Tyndall, Carolus Duran, Bastien-Lepage coven asserted that an artist or a poet must paint or write in the style of his own day, and this with 'The Fairy Queen,' and 'Lyrical Ballads,' and Blake's early poems in its ears, and plain to the eyes, in book or gallery, those great masterpieces of later Egypt, founded upon that work of the Ancient Kingdom already further in time from later Egypt than later Egypt is from us. I knew that I could choose my style where I pleased, that no man can deny to the human mind any power, that power once achieved; and yet I did not wish to recover the first simplicity. If I must be but a shepherd building his hut among the ruins of some fallen city, I might take porphyry or shaped marble, if it lay ready to my hand, instead of the baked clay of the first builders. If Chaucer's personages had disengaged themselves from Chaucer's crowd, forgotten their common goal and shrine, and after sundry magnifications become, each in his turn, the centre of some Elizabethan play, and a few years later split into their elements, and so given birth to romantic poetry, I need not reverse the cinematograph. I could take those separated elements, all that abstract love and melancholy, and give them a symbolical or mythological coherence. Not Chaucer's rough-tongued riders, but some procession of the Gods! a pilgrimage no more but perhaps a shrine! Might I not, with health and good luck to aid me, create some new 'Prometheus Unbound,' Patrick or Columbcille, Oisin or Fion, in Prometheus's stead, and, instead of Caucasus, Croagh-Patrick or Ben Bulben? Have not all races had their first unity from a polytheism that marries them to rock and hill? We had in Ireland imaginative stories, which the uneducated classes knew and even sang, and might we not make those stories current among the educated classes, re-discovering for the work's sake what I have called 'the applied arts of literature,' the association of literature, that is, with music, speech and dance; and at last, it might be, so deepen the political passion of the nation that all, artist and poet, craftsman and day labourer would accept a common design? Perhaps even these images, once created and associated with river and mountain, might move of themselves, and with some powerful even turbulent life, like those painted horses that trampled the rice fields of Japan.

XXII

I used to tell the few friends to whom I could speak these secret thoughts that I would make the attempt in Ireland but fail, for our civilisation, its elements multiplying by divisions like certain low forms of life, was all powerful; but in reality I had the wildest hopes. To-day I add to that first conviction, to that first desire for unity, this other conviction, long a mere opinion vaguely or intermittently apprehended: Nations, races and individual men are unified by an image, or bundle of related images, symbolical or evocative of the state of mind, which is of all states of mind not impossible, the most difficult to that man, race or nation; because only the greatest obstacle that can be contemplated without despair rouses the will to full intensity. A powerful class by terror, rhetoric, and organised sentimentality, may drive their people to war, but the day draws near when they cannot keep them there; and how shall they face the pure nations of the East when the day comes to do it with but equal arms? I had seen Ireland in my own time turn from the bragging rhetoric and gregarious humour of O'Connell's generation and school, and offer herself to the solitary and proud Parnell as to her anti-self, buskin following hard on sock; and I had begun to hope, or to half-hope, that we might be the first in Europe to seek unity as deliberately as it had been sought by theologian, poet, sculptor, architect from the eleventh to the thirteenth century. Doubtless we must seek it differently, no longer considering it convenient to epitomise all human knowledge, but find it we well might, could we first find philosophy and a little passion.

XXIII

It was the death of Parnell that convinced me that the moment had come for work in Ireland, for I knew that for a time the imagination of young men would turn from politics. There was a little Irish patriotic society of young people, clerks, shop-boys, shop-girls, and the like, called the Southwark Irish Literary Society. It had ceased to meet because each member of the committee had lectured so many times that the girls got the giggles whenever he stood up. I invited the committee to my father's house at Bedford Park and there proposed a new organisation. After a few months spent in founding, with the help of T. W. Rolleston, who came to that first meeting and had a knowledge of committee work I lacked, the Irish Literary Society, which soon included every London Irish author and journalist, I went to Dublin and founded there a similar society.

W. B. Yeats.